For Bobby and John, and to the good times.
Many thanks!
—A. W.

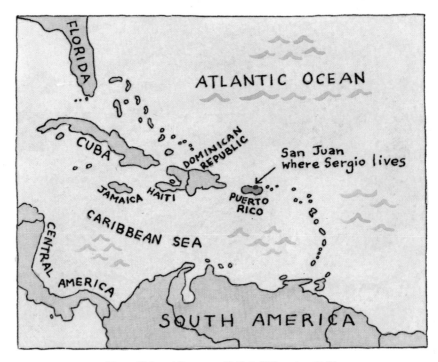

Henry Holt and Company, LLC, *Publishers since 1866*
115 West 18th Street, New York, New York 10011

Henry Holt is a registered trademark of Henry Holt and Company, LLC

Published in Canada by Fitzhenry & Whiteside Ltd.,
195 Allstate Parkway, Markham, Ontario L3R 4T8.

Library of Congress Cataloging-in-Publication Data
Wallner, Alexandra.
Sergio and the hurricane / by Alexandra Wallner.
Summary: A young boy is excited when he hears that a hurricane is coming to his oceanfront home
in San Juan, Puerto Rico, but when it comes, he learns how dangerous hurricanes can be.
[1. Hurricanes—Fiction.    2. Puerto Rico—Fiction.]    I. Title.
PZ7.W15938Sg   2000   [E]—dc21      99-40724

ISBN 0-8050-6203-3 / First Edition—2000 / Designed by Nicole Stanco
Printed in the United States of America on acid-free paper. ∞
The artist used gouache on 140-pound Arches
hot-press paper to create the illustrations for this book.
1   3   5   7   9   10   8   6   4   2

# Sergio and the Hurricane

## Alexandra Wallner

Henry Holt and Company · New York

ergio lived in San Juan, Puerto Rico, with his mama, papa, dog Peanut, and cat Misu in a cottage across the street from the ocean.

Every morning he sat on the beach with Peanut, watching the bright windsurfing boats sail on the turquoise water. But today the ocean was dark green, and the waves were too big and choppy for small boats.

"A storm must be coming," Sergio said, scratching Peanut's ear.

He walked to the small park down the street. Usually the park was full of people, but today there was no one. The air was hot. Sergio had just taken a shower, but already his skin felt sticky with sweat.

He bought an ice-cream cone at his friend Raffi's refreshment stand.

"Hurricane weather," Raffi said, frowning. "The TV says a huge storm is coming our way."

"I hope you're right!" Sergio said. He was too young to remember the last big hurricane that had hit San Juan, so he was excited.

"A hurricane is a very serious thing," said Raffi, still frowning.

Sergio ran home.

"Mama! Mama!" he cried. "Raffi says a hurricane is coming!"

"Yes, Sergio," said Mama. "I know. Hurry, we must go to the supermarket to get some supplies before the hurricane comes."

The supermarket was crowded. Sergio and Mama were not the only ones preparing for the hurricane.

As they drove home, they saw people boarding up windows with sheets of plywood or crisscrossing masking tape over them.

"Why are they doing that?" Sergio asked.

"To keep the glass from shattering and hurting people," Mama explained.

bottled water
flashlight batteries
radio batteries
candles + matches
canned fruit
canned vegetables
canned meat
canned soup
spaghetti
cereal
dry milk
crackers
soda
cookies
peanut butter~jelly
bread
cat food   dog food

Hurricane reports blared from car radios.

It's so exciting! Sergio thought.

When they got home, Papa was putting metal shutters over the windows.

"Papa! Papa!" Sergio cried, jumping up and down. "Do you think it will be a big hurricane?"

"A hurricane is a very serious thing," Papa said. "After you help Mama with the groceries, I will need your help outside."

Papa and Sergio put the outdoor furniture in the garage. Then Sergio watched Papa cut the coconuts off the palm trees in the yard. A high wind could throw the furniture and coconuts through the windows.

By the time everything was done, it was late afternoon. As Sergio and his parents ate dinner, rain began to drum on the roof. Sergio peeked through a crack in the shutters. Sand from the beach sliced across the road. Waves as tall as hills slammed the cement seawall across the street.

After the excitement of the day, Sergio was very tired. He fell asleep listening to the wind howl.

Sometime later, Sergio woke suddenly. The howling wind was rattling the shutters like it wanted to break in.

Sergio saw a candle burning on his dresser. The electricity must have gone out! He felt afraid all by himself, so he went into his parents' room and snuggled into bed with them.

They listened to the battery-powered radio. "Wind is gusting up to 170 miles per hour," a voice crackled. "Utility poles are snapping like matchsticks. Electricity is out all over San Juan and the east coast. Please, everyone, stay indoors until the hurricane is over!"

The hurricane was wild and noisy. It wasn't as much fun as Sergio had thought it was going to be.

"I'm scared," Sergio admitted, so Papa told him a story.

"The last time there was a really big hurricane like this was when your grandmother was young. She lived on a farm. The wind blew so hard that it scared the cow, who knocked over an oil lamp. The straw caught fire, but grandmother used some big cans of milk to put it out just in time to save the barn."

Papa's voice was warm and comforting, and Sergio fell asleep. When he woke up it was late morning. Peanut and Misu were still in bed with him, but his parents were gone.

"Mama, Papa, where are you?" he called, running to the kitchen.

"Hush, dear," Mama said, putting her arms around him. "The hurricane is over. Let's go outside to see what happened."

The sun was shining and the ocean was calm, almost as if there had never been a hurricane. But there was a lot of damage. Flying sand had blasted the pink paint off the front of the cottage. The palm trees had knocked some tiles off the roof.

Sergio's family would have to do a lot of work, but not as much as the neighbors. Old Mr. Gonzalez's banyan tree, which was older than Mr. Gonzalez himself, had uprooted and crashed into his house.

Along the street, trees and utility poles had fallen and crashed into fences, houses, and cars. Water flooded the streets where drainpipes were clogged.

Slowly, carefully, Sergio walked to the park. Most of the palm trees had lost their leaves, and some had broken in half. Raffi was looking sadly at the heap of rubble that had been his stand. "It will take a lot of money to build a new one," he said, sighing.

That afternoon, Sergio went to the beach with Peanut and played in the water. The beach was full of people. Everyone in San Juan had the day off, but no one was smiling. It would take a lot of time and hard work to clean up the mess the hurricane had made.

There was no electricity. The pumps that brought water to the city were not working. Instead, a truck brought fresh water in big plastic bottles to Sergio's street.

"Help me carry fresh water
from the truck," Mama said.

"Help me carry water from
the ocean so we can flush the
toilets," Papa said.

"Pick up the dead branches
around the house," Mama said.

"Help me shovel the sand
from the yard," Papa said.

At the end of the day, Sergio felt very dirty. "May I take a bath?" he asked. "No, dear, only a sponge bath," Mama said. "We must only use this water for drinking and cooking."

A few nights later it rained hard. Sergio and his parents ran into the backyard with soap and shampoo and took long showers. That felt good!

For many weeks, men cut up the trees that had fallen into power lines. Then, one day, electricity flowed through the wires again.

A few days later, water came out of the faucets. School started, and Mrs. Hernandez, Sergio's teacher, gave the class a science lesson on hurricanes.

After many months, most people had repaired and painted their houses and cleaned up their streets. They were happy again, and things were back to normal.

One day, Papa asked, "Will you ever forget the hurricane, Sergio?"
"No, Papa," he said. "And I will never ever wish for one again."

# Facts About Hurricanes

Hurricanes start in tropical oceans when the temperature of the water near the surface is 80 degrees Fahrenheit or more. The warm water evaporates and becomes vapor. Changes in the air pressure cause the vapor to move in a circular pattern, which creates wind. The vapor turns into small drops of water, and heat is released.

This warm air rises in a column and is now called a cyclone. When the cyclone grows, clouds are formed, causing rain and thunderstorms. Some cyclones die quickly, but others develop into hurricanes. If a cyclone's winds reach more than 74 miles per hour, it is called a hurricane.

The calm area in the middle of the hurricane is called its eye. Heavy rain comes from clouds surrounding the eye, yet in the eye the sky is clear and the winds are mild.

Hurricanes can last for just a few hours or for as long as two weeks. They die down when they pass over land or cooler parts of the ocean and there's no more warm water to feed them.

The damage hurricanes cause can be serious. Winds can tear down buildings, topple trees and power lines, throw objects around, and cause the ocean to flood. Too much rain in a short period of time can also cause flooding.

A hurricane can't be stopped, but pictures sent from weather satellites can tell people when one is coming. Then they can try to prevent damage just as the people in Sergio's neighborhood did.